BEING BIG S

Im a big
sister now.

Written and Illustrated by
Priya Ram

Lilly likes to watch her mom's **belly**.
It moves and jiggles just like **jelly**.

She's been waiting to meet her sibling so **bad.**
"Just wait for a few more weeks," says **dad.**

The crib is ready, and there are new baby **clothes**,
A colorful mobile and a pair of socks for baby's **toes.**

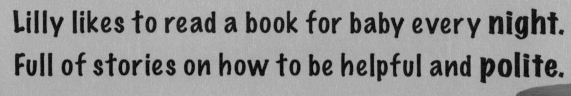

Lilly likes to read a book for baby every **night**.
Full of stories on how to be helpful and **polite**.

Dad has made a list of **tasks**.
"Are they all for me?" Lilly **asks**.

Dad says, "Lilly you are now **grown**."
"You can learn to do things on your **own**."

Lilly asks, "I wonder what a baby is like?"
"Can baby wear a helmet and ride a bike?"

"Can baby **sing**
or play the guitar **string?**"

"Can baby kick a **ball**
and make sure not to **fall?**"

Dad says that babies are very **small**.

First, they learn how to roll...

...and then **crawl**.

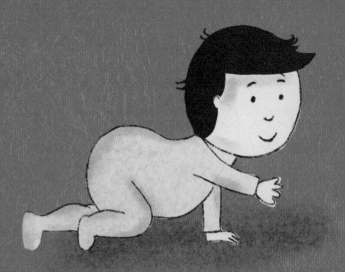

But they can play with us when they are **tall**.

The long wait is finally over!

Someone special
has come over.

Baby has tiny eyes and **nose,**

Hair so soft and ten small **toes.**

Baby is cute as a **kitten.**

Lilly is surely **smitten.**

Baby often needs mom's milk to **drink**,
Dad helps to cook and cleans up the **sink**.

Shining with colorful red and green **light,**
The monitor lets Lilly know if baby is **alright.**

Baby wakes up, cries for milk every night.
So, Lilly sleeps in her room, tucked in **tight**.

When they go for a walk, Lilly pushes the **stroller**.
She says, "I'm a big sister, and I want to be **stronger**."

Lilly gives cuddles that are warm and **cozy**.
It helps to calm down when baby is **fussy**.

Every day they like to spend some time **together**.
It's when they show their love for **each other**.

Other times, it's good to play and be on your **own**,
It gives mom and dad some time to be **alone**.

Lilly gets to teach and guide the little **one**.
She shows how things are properly **done**.

She helps with baby in so many **ways.**
She tries to be the best sister **always!**

Baby is growing so **fast**.
The family is having a **blast**.
There's lots of joy and **giggling**.
Lilly is grateful for her **sibling!**

Printed in Great Britain
by Amazon

45133809R00016